The Friendship Fairies

The Friendship Fairies

LUCY KENNEDY

ILLUSTRATED BY
PHILLIP CULLEN

Gill Books

Gill Books
Hume Avenue
Park West
Dublin 12

www.gillbooks.ie

Gill Books is an imprint of M.H. Gill and Co.

Text © Lucy Kennedy 2019, 2020
Illustrations © Phillip Cullen 2019, 2020
First published in hardback 2019
First published in paperback 2020

978 07171 8949 6

Printed by BZ Graf S.A., Poland
This book is typeset in Baskerville.

The paper used in this book comes from the wood pulp
of managed forests. For every tree felled, at least one
tree is planted, thereby renewing natural resources.

A CIP catalogue record for this book is available from
the British Library.

CONTENTS

To my very best friends:

Richard

Jack

Holly and Jess

xxx

CHAPTER ONE

'Last one out is a total troll!' said Holly Dixon.

Bright-eyed and full of mischief, the cheeky fairy had curly brown hair tied up in pigtails and her shoelaces were untied. Holly was a complete messer, but she had a clever twinkle in her brown eyes. She could put on funny accents to make her family laugh, and her best ones were American or Scottish. She also told rude jokes that sometimes got her into big trouble with her parents.

'We're coming,' said Emme, flying down the stairs of their wooden treehouse with little Jess trailing behind her. They had just finished brushing their teeth, and Jess had toothpaste in her hair.

'It's day one of the Kindness Course,' said Emme, 'and I really, really want to graduate this week! We need to mind our manners.' Emme was the oldest, most sensible sister in the Dixon family. She had a serious face and big eyes, and she liked people to stick to the rules. Holly called her a nerd, but she didn't care – she thought that nerds were actually pretty cool. She loved going to school every day, and was particularly looking forward to this week. If she passed the Kindness Course, she would be well on her way to becoming a fully qualified Friendship Fairy.

'You don't have manners when you **buuuurp**, Jess!' said Holly, laughing loudly and then snorting by mistake.

'I do not burp,' said Jess, crossly. Her hair was fair, her eyes were very blue, and she always had rosy cheeks. She was the smallest of the three sisters. She gave everyone great big cuddles, but when she was cross, you wouldn't want to mess with her! Jess also liked to 'borrow' her sisters' things. But because she was the baby of the family, she often got away with it.

The three fairy sisters lived in a treehouse with a bright pink door and beautiful window baskets spilling over the four sash windows. A wonky chimney poked up out of the roof and into the leaves. At night-time, if it wasn't raining, the top of the treehouse could open so they could see the stars.

Inside, there were six rooms: a big bright yellow kitchen, a cosy playroom, a sitting room with rainbows painted on the walls, a big bathroom, Mr and Mrs Dixon's tidy bedroom, and the bedroom that the three girls shared.

In their room, there were three bunk beds attached to the curved wall of the treehouse. Each bunk was like a little cocoon, so they could see the starry sky as they were falling asleep. Holly had lots of dolls at the end of her bed. She knew all their names and talked to them every night. Some of them were cute, and some were a bit manky, but she loved them all equally.

As they were leaving for school, Emme had
to remind Holly that her packed lunch was in the
fridge. Today the girls were having gnome-shaped
pasta with secret tomato sauce and an apple each.
They only drank rainwater to keep their teeth
nice and white, and, as a
treat, fairberry juice.
Fairberries were a
cross between a kiwi, a
blackberry and a peach. They were ugly, hairy and
smelled a little like feet, but they made the most
delicious juice. They grew on vines all around the
neighbourhood.

The three fairies flew off together, their
backpacks slung over their shoulders, laughing and
pretending to push each other. The sisters were
close – they didn't argue (too much) and they tried

to stick together. Their parents always told the girls that family comes first and that it was important to look after each other, no matter what.

They had lots of neighbours – the family of Mexican elves who were renting a treehouse for a year; the party ants who played loud music every night; and Mr and Mr Snail, a lovely old couple who couldn't see very well, but they always insisted on walking across the road first, making everyone behind them late!

But right next door, in number 8 Tree Road, lived their number-one enemies, the **Barns Boys**. Ollie, Hugo and Harry were triplets and they were very, very naughty. A few weeks ago, they had covered a hole in the tree with grass, put a delicious chewy jelly on top, and then hid behind the fence. When Holly saw the glistening sweet, she snuck over to eat it and fell right into the hole! She was furious (but she still ate the jelly).

That day, Hugo was sticking his bum out of the window at the people passing by. Emme was disgusted and gave out to him, but he told her to butt out! At least we don't have to see them for the rest of the day, thought Emme.

The boys were a little bit older, so they went to the secondary school, where you could choose all sorts of different subjects.

Their tree was right in the middle of a park surrounded by a fairy fort that had been there for hundreds and hundreds of years. When the tree was planted, a wise leprechaun had put a spell on it. If a human came too close, a shimmering film would sprout from the top of the tree to cover the neighbourhood and protect it.

If the magical creatures were seen by humans, they would lose some of their powers and would have to go to Tír na nÓg, the Irish-speaking caravan park, to recharge. The girls found the journey really long, and the food was rotten there, so they tried their best not to be seen.

The only exception was children. If children saw them, they would be safe, because children had the same type of hearts as fairies. That's why the children believed in them, their magic and their world. Adults were so busy trying to work out the magic that they missed it.

CHAPTER TWO

At the bottom of the tree was the Magic Manor, a school were the young pupils learnt everything from eating politely to flushing the loo properly.

The school had one hundred pupils made up of all types of magical creatures and animals. They also had exchange students from other countries, like the polar bear twins from Alaska, the camels from Lanzarote and the trolls from Sweden. The girls went there every morning. Afterwards, they had the afternoons off.

Their teacher, Ms Ava, was the coolest person they knew. She had a different hairstyle every day, and at weekends she put colours through her hair, like a unicorn. She was always smiling, and she knew just how to make the young students feel good about themselves.

They didn't really know anything else about her, though. Did she have a pet? Was she married? What did she do after work? They all wanted to find out … but today was not the day.

'Okay, everyone listen up,' said Ms Ava, clapping her hands. 'Today, the older pupils begin their Kindness Course. As you all know, you need to pass all four of the assignments to graduate.'

There was a buzz of excitement in the class. Ms Ava smiled at them. 'You can ask the younger students to help you – you know how much I love teamwork.' Emme looked at her sisters and winked. They were the best team she knew.

'So,' continued Ms Ava, 'this week we're going to cover four subjects. Today's one is **Gentle Hands**. This is a very important lesson. Who knows what it means?'

Jess put up her hand immediately, feeling very excited. 'I do! It's when you are gentle and caring with your hands, like this.' She stroked her face to show everyone. All the pupils smiled at her, and she blushed, making her cheeks even rosier, knowing that she had a captive audience. She also knew that she had 'borrowed' Emme's good sparkly pencil, so she made sure to keep that hidden!

'Exactly, Jess,' said Ms Ava. 'Why don't you all practise Gentle Hands with each other,' she suggested. With that, there were lots of high fives, fist bumping, hair brushing and hand shaking.

'Okay, you get the idea,' she said, laughing. 'Now, you can all go out and about the village and work on this. If you see a child hurting

someone else, you explain to them that they
need to show their Gentle Hands.'

Ms Ava closed her book and put it into
her teacher's bag. All of the pupils were
fascinated by this bag. It was purple and
shaped like a square box. It didn't look very
big, but it seemed to fit a lot of unusually large
things in it. Emme once saw Ms Ava take out
a full paddling pool when she was in the park.

woof!

The bag also barked like a small dog if anyone tried to get too close to it.

Ms Ava smiled to herself. She loved her job, but she was in a hurry because she was going on a secret date. She watched the class pack up their notebooks and bags and head off.

After they ate their lunch, the sisters flew through the park and into the local town, where the humans lived. It had plenty of shops. There was one that sold bikes, a bakery with sticky buns, a butcher's, a hairdresser's and the fairies' favourite shop – the sweetshop. It was called Goblin-it-Up, and it was the best sweetshop in the world.

The door handles were liquorice, the walls were lined with edible paper and the cash register was covered in bonbons. You could find every type of sweet there that you could imagine – tasty jellies, chocolate lollipops, giant gobstoppers, buckets of sherbet, fizzy cola bottles and chocolate in every colour.

Sometimes, when no one was looking,

Holly would go in, take a jelly and hide it in

her pigtails. Emme often wondered why the

bees loved Holly's hair so much … Jess just wondered where Holly stored all her disguises. Her bonkers sister liked to dress up differently the whole time to protect her identity, and today, she was putting on a baseball cap and a twisty moustache.

The three fairies hovered outside the shop, noses pressed right up against the glass. They were dreaming of the tasty, chewy sweets when Holly saw something happening inside.

'Oh look,' she said, nudging her sisters, 'this doesn't look good. I see a human child being as bold as a black bat.'

'Holly!' said Emme, in a cross whisper. It worried her that her younger sister didn't care about being rude. Lots of things worried her, but she tried to stay positive.

'What's going on?' asked Jess, trying to get to the front to get a better look. Their eyes followed Holly's pointing finger.

Inside the shop, there was a little boy and a girl. The girl had her brother's arm in a tight grip and the boy was doing crazy karate moves,

trying to chop her head off! They were making a lot of noise.

Their mum was chatting away to the lady behind the counter and she didn't notice anything.

'I have to dye my hair twice a month to cover the greys,' the mother was saying.

'Well, sometimes I just use a black pen and draw on my head,' the shopkeeper replied, and the mother looked quite surprised.

The little boy was now pulling the girl's hair and she even started to spit at him … things were getting serious.

'Oh no,' said Emme. 'Let's try to sort this out.' The girls flew quietly in the door and headed over to the shouting children. 'Excuse me,' said Emme, trying to get their attention.

But the children were fighting so much that they didn't even hear her.

'**Excuse me**,' said Emme a second time, a little less politely. 'What is going on here?'

The little girl stopped straight away and looked shocked to see three tiny fairies staring at her. She squinted her eyes and then rubbed them to make sure that she wasn't dreaming. She adored fairies and talked to them in her room, but she never thought until this very moment that they could actually be real.

'Umm ...' the little girl began slowly. She had noticed that one of the fairies had a moustache and was wearing a baseball cap, even though they were indoors. These fairies weren't what she had expected!

She tried again. 'Well, you see ... I wouldn't give him my pocket money because Mum said we aren't allowed sweets today,' the girl said. 'So he hit me. And I hit him back.' She folded her arms and stared at her brother with a cross face. He hadn't noticed the fairies yet – he was too busy running around, chasing his own shoe.

'Well' said Emme, in a kind, calm voice. 'If your mum said no, then no means no. What's your name?'

'Bella,' the little girl said, with her hands on her hips, 'and this naughty boy is my brother, Jack. He always wants to take my things, and it's not fair.'

'I know,' said Holly, staring straight at Jess. 'I have a little sister who likes to do that.'

Holly was remembering when Jess had put Sudocrem in her dolls' eyes and picked the stickers off her bed! Jess stuck out her tongue at her big sister.

Emme frowned at the other two and turned to Bella. 'You must remember that you are older, so you have to teach your little brother how to use his Gentle Hands.'

'Gentle Hands?' Bella was confused. 'What are they? Where do I get them from?'

'You already have them,' said Emme, pointing at her hands. 'They're your own hands, but you make sure that they are gentle.' Bella looked at her hands as if seeing them for the first time.

Jess explained. 'When using your hands, you must only ever help someone with them and never hurt them.' She showed Bella how to gently stroke her own face. 'Why don't you show your brother your Gentle Hands?'

'Okay,' said Bella. She called over to her brother. 'Jack, here are my Gentle Hands. Now show me yours.' Jack turned around and was speechless to see his sister talking to tiny fairies, especially one that was wearing a baseball cap.

He raised his hands slowly, without taking his eyes off the fairies.

'These are your very own Gentle Hands, and you should only use them to help, never hurt,' Bella said, putting her hand gently on his cheek.

Jack smiled because, even though they fought, he adored his big sister. He gave her a big hug. 'Gentle Hands, Gentle Hands, Gentle Hands,' he shouted, running noisily around the shop, flapping his arms like a bird trying to take off. The three fairies and Bella burst out laughing. 'At least he's using his hands for something other than hitting!' said Holly.

'What's going on here,' said their mother in a stern voice, finally turning around. 'What are you laughing at?'

'Well, Mum, the fairies told us how to have Gentle Hands,' said Jack, pointing his finger in the air ... but there was nothing there. All that was visible was a tiny baseball cap falling onto the ground, but Bella quickly kicked it under the counter. The sisters had disappeared.

'Fairies?' said their mother, laughing. 'Jack, you are a funny little boy, always coming up with crazy ideas.'

'Yes, Jack,' said Bella, winking at him. 'Fairies are not real.' They giggled together as they left the shop, holding each other's Gentle Hands.

'Phew,' said Holly, as the sisters flew home. 'That was a close one.' But as she put her hand to her head, she realised that her baseball cap was gone. 'My cap! I'm having a bad hair day!' she shouted, trying to fly back to the shop.

'No way, Hols, it's late,' said Emme. 'We'll collect it another day.'

Mr and Mrs Dixon were fun and fair, but they were strict about dinnertime. Also, Emme really wanted to watch *Tiny Dresser*, a show she loved. It was a programme about a witch who designed dresses for special occasions. This week, the crew were helping a female dinosaur prepare for her big wedding day. She was insisting on wearing a bikini top, and they were trying to change her mind!

'I've completed my first assignment and I couldn't have done it as well without you two. Thank you, guys.' Emme had a rush of love for her sisters. She knew how lucky she was that they all got on well. Some of her friends fought with their brothers and sisters the whole time.

'You're very welcome,' said Holly, totally seriously, putting out her hand. 'You can pay us in cash, please.'

The girls all laughed as they reached their front door, tired but happy. Emme filled in her homework and ticked the box marked Assignment one: Successful. She gave it to Bob, their family pigeon, who flew off to Ms Ava's house.

The girls had dinner with their parents, went for their baths and had an early night.

As they looked at the stars, Jess sang 'geeeentle haaaands' loudly twelve times and ended up with a pillow in the head from Holly.

CHAPTER THREE

The next day, Holly woke up early by mistake, because she hadn't set her alarm clock properly. It was a bright morning, so she thought that it would be nice to make their lunches … and, more importantly, do some spying!

Holly was very messy. She flung everything all over the kitchen, and some jam even ended up on the roof. But she managed to pack their lunch without breaking anything and set the three lunchboxes full of jam sambos, a yoghurt and a pear near their backpacks.

Then it was time to check on the Barns
Boys. Last week, she had seen one of
the triplets, Harry, trying to help Mr
Snail cross the road. She was
beginning to dislike
him a little less. But his
brothers Ollie and Hugo
wrecked her head, and
when the triplets were
together, trouble would follow. Time to
see if they were planning anything.

Holly put on her full camouflage gear,
including a helmet, and climbed outside to
the roof. She couldn't just fly over, because even
though humans can't hear it, fairies' wings make a
soft buzzing noise. All fairies have super-sensitive
hearing, and it would be embarrassing and bad for

her reputation if the Barns Boys caught her.

Very quietly, she leapt over to the next branch and clung on. She took out her rope, attached it to a twig and started to abseil down. She lowered herself beside the bedroom window …

… and tried not to laugh when she saw the three lads in the same big bed, snoring and farting, all dressed like dinosaurs.

Just then, she heard movement in her own treehouse, so she grabbed the rope, swung back up to the trunk and jumped over to her own roof. She quickly changed, hid her bag of disguises in a hole in the branch, and flew to the kitchen window as quietly as she could.

'What's going on?' said Emme, shocked to see that Holly was, first of all, awake, and second, outside the window!

'Ah, top of the morning to you,' said Holly in an American accent. She was a bit out of breath. 'I ... em ... well, I set my alarm early to try some yoga on a cloud, to stretch ... '

Emme knew she was lying, but Holly's crazy schemes made her laugh, so she didn't tell her sister that her dress was inside-out! 'Well done, Hols, I'm very impressed. Thank you for making our lunches.'

Jess came down the stairs, with toothpaste in her hair again, and, after breakfast, they all flew off to school together. As they passed the treehouse next door, the Barns Boys were up and leaning on their fence.

'Knock, knock,' Ollie shouted.

'Who's there?' said Holly.

'Imap,' said Ollie, smirking.

'Imap who?' said Holly and then groaned when she realised what she had just said.

'Ignore them,' said Emme, with her head held high in a posh way. 'It's not worth explaining good manners to them.' How they

had passed their Kindness Course, Emme

would never know!

Jess waved at the boys sweetly and, when the other two sisters weren't looking, Holly pulled a face at them. She had plans for those annoying boys!

In school, Ms Ava looked even more lovely than usual. Her curly brown hair was in a bun and she was wearing lipstick.

'You look lovely, Miss,' said Emme, dying to know why their teacher was wearing fancy makeup. But Holly called out, 'Going on a date, are we?' and Emme nearly fainted with embarrassment.

The whole class stopped talking in shock. You could hear a pin drop.

'Holly, you should never ask a lady personal questions,' said Ms Ava, trying not to smile. If only her class knew what she was doing later.

She clapped her hands. 'Okay, everyone, it's day two of our Kindness Course. Today we are going to look at **Kind Feet**. Does anyone know what this means?'

The whole class looked very confused, and no one put up their hand. There was lots of whispering and some people stared at their feet.

'Right,' said Ms Ava, laughing. 'Kind Feet is where you use your feet in kind ways. It means keeping your feet to yourself – this means no kicking or stomping. Can everyone show me Kind Feet?' The whole class tucked their feet gently under the tables, even the camels.

Ms Ava looked around the classroom and smiled at the little faces watching her in concentration. They were mostly a good class, except for one or two bold fairies who were tyrants. The camels were very windy and, unfortunately, farted a lot after breakfast. The class had to keep the window open but also keep an eye on the polar bear twins, who would try

to ski down the side of the building when the
teacher wasn't looking.

But Ms Ava really wanted the older ones to
graduate. 'If you see anybody using their feet

in an unkind way, you need to sort this out.
This is your second assignment.' Her students
nodded back at her. 'Good luck today,
everyone,' she added.

Off the sisters flew, chatting and waving at their friends. It was Tuesday, so they decided to go to their park for an ice-cream. There were lots of knotholes on the trunk of their tree. The top three holes led to a cinema, a funfair and a toyshop, and the bottom one led to Tasty Green.

Every Tuesday, there was a huge ice-cream

fountain in the middle of the green. The fountain

poured down delicious flavours like marshmallow

magic, sweet lemon, chocolate twinkle, chewy

toffee and vanilla ice. Everyone was given a small,

cup-shaped leaf when they flew in and they could

fill it with whatever ice-cream they liked.

Holly picked strawberry cream, Emme

chose vanilla ice and Jess picked mint chocolate,

and they sat down to eat them. Holly put on a huge pair of black sunglasses. She liked to look cool even when she was relaxing in the park on a cloudy afternoon. 'What a beautiful day,' said Emme, who always tried to be positive about everything, including the weather!

They looked around the park as they ate their ice-creams. Fairies were walking their pet dragonflies, a family of elves was playing football and there was a little group of tiny caterpillars on a school trip.

Then Emme heard something outside the tree. The noise sounded like it was coming from outside Tasty Green, in the human world. Fairies' hearing could stretch for miles, which was annoying when there were human concerts on. She much preferred to listen to her favourite band, The Twisters.

'Come on, guys,' Emme said to her sisters, as they put their ice-cream cups into the compost heap. They flew out of the tree hole, across the park and over to the main road.

As they got closer, Emme could see the problem. Two boys were kicking each other and one of them had a bleeding nose. Beside them on the ground were their scooters.

'No, I won,' the boy with the brown hair was shouting.

'No you didn't, you're a cheater, cheater, pickle eater,' said the fair-haired one, aiming a kick at the other boy's knee, missing and kicking the scooter instead.

'I didn't cheat, I was just faster!' said the other boy. He took off his helmet and rubbed his eyes. He was very upset that his brother

was lying. He knew that he had won the race fair and square.

'Can we help you at all?' said Emme, as the three sisters flew over. The boys were too busy kicking each other roughly to hear her.

'**Helllooo**, boys, we're up here!' called Holly mischievously. Emme gave her a look which said to stop messing. She tried again. 'Excuse me, we see that you are fighting. Can we help?'

This time, the brown-haired boy looked up. His mouth dropped as he saw three little fairies all looking at him, with their wings fluttering. 'Who are you?' he asked, looking around to see if anyone else could see what he was seeing.

'We are park security,' said Holly, crossing her arms. She had put on a tie, and, with her sunglasses, she looked more like a bodyguard

than a fairy. Emme shook her head. Why was her sister acting so weird?

'Actually, we're fairies, and we want to help children to be kind. What's your name?' said Jess.

'Bobby,' the boy said. 'But why are you talking to me?'

'We saw that you were kicking this boy here,' said Emme, pointing to the sad fair-haired boy.

'That's because my brother Johnny said that I was cheating, but I wasn't.' Bobby looked embarrassed.

'Have you heard of Kind Feet?' asked Emme.

'No, I don't think so,' said Bobby.

'Well, this means that you only use your feet to walk or run with, not to kick or hurt someone.'

'You're not a donkey, dude,' Holly added.

'Thank you, Holly,' said Emme, giving her sister another look. Holly looked embarrassed and took off her sunglasses. 'So,' said Emme. 'Can you say sorry to your brother now?'

So, with that, Bobby walked over to Johnny and said sorry to him. Johnny accepted his apology, like only brothers can. They shook hands, put their helmets back on and agreed that they were being silly. They used their Kind Feet to scoot off together.

'Another point earned,' said Emme, high-fiving her sisters. 'That's two so far. But Holly, you must be more polite. You can't call people rude names!'

'Emme, I really think you need to …' Holly put her massive black sunglasses back on, '… chill. Maybe you need some more ice-cream,' she said and flew off laughing.

'Did she just snort again?' said Emme to Jess.

'Yep,' said Jess. 'That's our sister.' They flew off to catch up with Holly, who was doing somersaults in the air.

That evening, the girls baked some beautiful cream-filled fairy buns for Ms Ava. Holly had decided that she would try to bribe the nice triplet, Harry, with a bun, to get some information on his brothers.

Mr Dixon was a brilliant pastry chef. He taught cooking in a culinary school, so the girls learned lots of good tips and recipes from him. He could make absolutely anything out of flour, fairy dust and a song. He would sing to help the ingredients mix together – and it worked. Like magic, the

spoon would turn as he hit the higher notes.
He was so good, in fact, that the *Fairy Good
Bake Off* wanted him on the show.

Mrs Dixon was home from work early too.
She was on a secret mission at the moment

– her job was to keep an eye on humans' behaviour. Humans didn't care about nature and the environment as much as they should, so the Fairy Council had set up a special unit. At the moment, humans were cutting down too many trees in their park, so her job was to spy on the workers and inform the engineers, who would then tamper with their forestry equipment. This had been going on for months and was successful so far – they had saved twenty trees!

After they finished baking, Emme filled in her homework and Bob the pigeon flew off to Ms Ava's house. For dinner, they had star-shaped fish nuggets. They all played Guess Who's Invisible around the kitchen table and they managed to complete the game without any tears. Well, almost – Jess was caught cheating by hiding on the roof again!

CHAPTER FOUR

'Day three, everybody,' said Ms Ava. 'Sit down now, please, and settle quietly.' All the students took out their books. Emme had drawn her favourite band on the cover of her notebook using glitter and sequins. The Twisters wore a lot of black and were super cool. All the other students admired the cover.

'Okay, today's assignment is called **Flush, Wash and Never Rush**. It's about using the bathroom properly,' said Ms Ava.

'Ah now, that's really gross, how disgusting,' said Holly, sitting back in her chair. Anything to do with toilet talk made her feel quite sick.

Jess giggled. She knew that this subject annoyed her sister, so sometimes she didn't flush the loo – just to see her reaction!

Ms Ava laughed. 'Yes, Holly, but many children don't do this right, and it is very bad manners. Flushing the toilet properly and cleaning your hands can keep away germs and help you stay healthy.' Holly shook her head and made a face.

'Jess, can you show people how to wash their hands properly, please,' asked Ms Ava.

Jess stood up confidently and walked over to the classroom sink. 'Just like this,' she said, turning on the tap and turning around to show everyone.

'Now Jess, you forgot the soap. Your hands are just wet, not clean,' said Ms Ava gently. 'You've just given the germs a nice bath!'

'Oh yes!' said Jess, going red. She squirted some soap on her hands, rubbed them together and then washed her hands with warm water.

For the rest of the morning, the class practised. The trolls couldn't quite get used to the idea of washing, so it had to be explained to them again. The classroom was covered in

water from all the practise and one of the poor Spanish camels got soap up his nose.

'Now,' said Ms Ava, eventually. 'I need you all to keep an eye out this afternoon and see if you see a child forget to flush and wash. And watch out for germs!' Because fairies were so small, they were very good at spotting tiny germs.

So with their new assignment in mind, off the class went, flying in lots of different directions. Some fairies headed to the human school, others to the village.

Emme thought that maybe they could go to the local pool. It was a damp Wednesday afternoon, so that was probably where most children would be. This was quite a dangerous place for the sisters, though. The fairies had to be very careful not to get too close. Their wings were so light that if they got a drop of pool water on one, it would weigh them down. Also, the chlorine that humans used to keep the water clean could take some colour off their lovely wings. Tie-dyed wings weren't fashionable, so Holly was especially worried!

But before they reached the pool, Emme spotted an empty bird's nest on the top of a low roof. Part of being a fairy meant looking after everybody, even when they didn't know it, and this included birds and animals. Jess especially didn't like seeing plastic all over the place, and she worried about the environment.

Together, the girls cleaned up the bird's nest by taking out the rubbish and plaiting some twigs to make it more secure. Jess collected

leaves and flowers and made some pillows and
a sheltered area. Now, when the bird laid some
eggs, they would be safe and comfortable.

'Much better,' said Jess, proud of her work.

Jess felt very connected to nature.

When she was older, she was going to build a nest and live in it with her feathered friends. She didn't like it when humans hurt the earth.

She once got her friend Oscar the robin to poo on a human's head in the park because he'd left plastic rubbish on the bench.

'Now where do we go, Emme?' Jess was really looking forward to seeing Holly's reaction to the toilets! They flew over to the main building

and looked in the window. The pool was packed
with children and families swimming together.
It was very noisy but looked like great fun.

Beside the baby pool there was a restaurant,
and that was where Emme led them.

The restaurant was half inside and half outside
and full of lots of brightly coloured tables and
chairs. The smells coming from the kitchen were

making Jess feel a bit hungry, so when no one was looking, she stole a chip!

The girls landed very quietly on the back of a chair and waited for a child to pass them to go into the bathroom.

'I actually can't believe that we're doing this,' said Holly, crossing her arms in disgust. 'It's probably the worst assignment in the actual world.'

'Here we go,' said Emme, getting excited. A child wearing armbands and dripping with water walked by. He passed the fairies and went into the toilet. 'Let's follow him.'

Quickly and quietly, the girls flew in and waited outside the door. Holly was furious and refused to look at anyone. Jess kept on catching Emme's eye and giggling because they knew how annoyed Holly was!

After a few minutes, the child opened the door to leave, and he was in a big rush to get back to the pool. The girls flew over to him and Holly put up her hand like a policewoman stopping traffic. She had taken some rubber gloves from her pocket and put them on because she did not want to get too close to the germs in the bathroom. She also had a chicken-head hat on because she couldn't find her police one.

The boy looked up at this little fairy and gulped in fright. What was going on here?

'Excuse me,' said Jess kindly, seeing that the boy was a bit upset. 'What's your name? Did you flush the toilet and then wash your hands?'

'Um …' the little boy stammered. 'My name is Charlie. I don't think so. No, I didn't.

Are you here to arrest me?' He'd left his glasses beside the pool so he couldn't quite make out whether he was talking to a person or a chicken. He kept blinking.

'Well, Charlie, a toilet carries lots of yucky germs and if you don't flush and wash your hands, it can spread them and make you sick.'

The boy seemed distracted. He was dying to get back into the pool with his friends, and he started to slip away.

'**WAIT**,' said Holly. 'Let me tell you about the germs I can see. There's big ones, and long ones, and spiky ones, and hairy ones, and spotty ones, and puffy ones, and …'

The boy flinched and made a face. 'Also,' said Holly, getting more and more into it, 'some germs crawl up your back and live in your

hair for ever. They are called the … um …
backcrawlies.'

'Okay!' said Charlie. 'I promise I'll wash my hands. I don't like the sound of those backcrawlies!'

So, with that, the boy went back into the bathroom. Emme followed and watched him flush the toilet. Then he squirted some soap on his hands, washed them and dried them. He even showed her how clean they were afterwards.

'Well done,' Emme said, as they came out together. Her sisters were nowhere to be seen. Then, from the corner of her eye, she saw that Jess was trying to balance another chip on her head and Holly was looking into a glass window and brushing her hair. What were they thinking!

Emme cleared her throat loudly and gave them a stern, unimpressed look. They flew over quickly. 'Oh good, Charlie,' said Jess, carrying on the conversation as if she'd been there all along. 'You must try and remember to Flush, Wash and Never Rush.'

'Okay,' he said, spotting his friends and running out to the pool. Every day he was surrounded by bossy ladies, he thought to himself. His mummy, his two sisters and now some tiny flying people!

'Nice one, team,' said Jess smiling at her sisters. Emme rolled her eyes.

'I'm just glad that I didn't have to go into the toilet,' said Holly, looking quite green.

They all laughed and headed home. On the way, Holly stopped for a chat with Harry, the nice triplet. He seemed a bit sad. His brothers had been slagging him because he had puked on his runners after playing a fairy sport. It involved flying upside down while trying to score goals with an acorn, but Harry always got dizzy.

Soon enough, though, Holly had him cheered up, and they were laughing together at her impression of her dad singing with his eyes closed! She handed him one of the cream buns they had baked, and he whispered something in her ear.

Emme didn't notice.

Assignment three: Complete. She was

well on her way to graduating now.

CHAPTER FIVE

'Yes, Ms Ava,' said the class in unison.

They were all actually a bit tired. These assignments were pretty full-on!

'So our fourth assignment is … **Sharing is Caring**. You all know this, but human children don't, so sometimes they need a reminder.'

Jess tried not to look in Holly's direction. She was making a point of staring at the ceiling suspiciously. That morning, the girls had got into massive trouble with their dad when the honeybee called in with her weekly delivery.

Every Thursday, she would drop in little yellow teacups full of delicious fresh honey. That morning, Holly had hidden the honey so she wouldn't have to share with Jess. Holly looked over at Jess and narrowed her eyes.

The class got to work. The polar bear twins also had a problem with sharing. They were so used to getting two of everything and not having to share. They started off by sharing their vegetable salad, but then one bit the other on the chin by mistake.

When they had finished practising their very best sharing, Ms Ava clapped her hands. 'Off you go, class, and keep your eyes peeled for non-sharers. Once you've completed today, you can go home and get an early night, as Friday is a big day!'

Ms Ava looked at their determined little faces. Unfortunately, not all of them would get medals tomorrow – but there was always next time.

Ms Ava headed off. She had lots of work ahead of her to organise the graduation. She had to collect the medals, send out the messenger pigeons and she had all the decorations to plan. The wizard chef, Mr Gloop (some mean fairies called him Mr Poop behind his back) would need to get the ingredients ready this evening. He was quite grumpy, so he liked lots of time to prepare.

After lunch, the three sisters made their way out of the school. 'Hip hip hooray,' sang Emme. She was so excited about the graduation tomorrow. She had her outfit picked out in her head ... but she was starting to feel a bit worried.

Maybe she'd made mistakes? Maybe Bob hadn't delivered her forms? Maybe she wasn't good enough? She tried to have positive thoughts and push any negative ones out of her head. That's what her dad had taught her – his favourite saying was: *Just when the caterpillar thought the world was ending, it turned into a butterfly.*

'Where are we off to today, boss?' asked Holly as she flew.

'I was actually thinking that for this assignment, I could just spend the morning with you two,' said Emme grinning. Her sisters could do with learning a thing or two about sharing!

'Very funny,' said Jess, rolling her eyes.

'Okay, how about the library?' suggested Emme. There was an arts and crafts section in the library so it should be busy with young children.

'Good call,' said Holly, putting on some serious glasses and wrapping her hair in a tight bun. Today she was going for the librarian look, so she added a pencil to the hair.

The sisters flew down on to the red-brick building that was the local library and, sure enough, it looked very busy. At the very end of the reading area was the arts and crafts section. Children of all ages loved it here because there

was a huge selection of art supplies – jumbo pom-poms, glitter glue, cotton wool in every colour and lots of fancy sniffy paper and pens.

The little fairies settled in behind some books and sat down. 'What are you going to

do when you graduate, Emme?' asked Jess
curiously. Even though she would miss hanging
out with her in school, she was proud of her big
sister for working so hard. She knew
that Emme hoped to become a

teacher when she left school, so moving on to the next school was important.

'I'm going to do something important. I'm going to help other fairies and I'm going to find some human children who we can trust to help the fairy world. Children who believe in us and who believe in what's right. They can help us fix some problems.' Emme's big eyes shone with excitement.

Before she could explain further, Holly shouted from behind her bright pink telescope. 'We have a situation – stage left!'

Emme and Jess looked to the left, confused, but there was nothing there. 'No,' said Holly, 'the other left!' They followed Holly's finger, and, sure enough, there was a commotion at one of the tables, where six children were sitting.

Two little girls were pulling each other's

hair, shouting and crying, all at the same time.

'I want the blue pen,' said one little girl.

'No, I need the blue pen,' shouted the other.
The table was full of every colour pen in the
world, and they were still fighting!

'Girls, girls, **GIRLS**!' said Holly, blocking
her ears and tutting. 'My ears! You sound like
cats screeching! Enough already.'

But Holly had raised her voice too much. All six pairs of eyes were now on them as the children looked up in shock. They were speechless.

'Um, hello,' said Holly, in a whisper, aware that she had almost blown their cover. 'Why are you fighting?'

The two girls said nothing, just stared, and held the blue pen tightly between them.

'Girls, you must learn how to share,' said Emme kindly. 'Sharing is caring, and that means that when you share, you show that you care.'

'Now put the pen down!' said Holly, and the little girls did what they were told. They were not going to mess with this crazy flying person with a giant pencil in her hair!

'Well done,' said Emme. 'So always remember that …?'

'Sharing is Caring,' the whole table said together. 'Job done,' thought Emme. 'That was simple!' Now it was time to make a quick exit. Holly threw a small seed pod in the corner of the room, which exploded with a loud bang. All the children jumped and looked behind them, which gave the sisters a chance to fly off.

'Guys, I need a hand with this,' said Jess, out of breath. The blue pen was on her shoulders, and she looked very unbalanced!

Emme was horrified. 'Jess, put that back – you can't take it!'

'Well, I thought it would stop them fighting,' she said, embarrassed.

'No. They have to learn how to share, so put it back, please,' said Emme. Jess did what she was told, reluctantly. It wasn't as easy to share as she'd first thought!

Later that night, Emme filled in her homework. She gave it to Bob, who'd brought his girlfriend with him, and they both flew off to Ms Ava's house.

She then sat on her bed watching the clock, waiting to see if Ms Ava's pigeon would deliver an invitation to the graduation.

She was so nervous that the time seemed to drag on for ever. She kept repeating her dad's saying: *Just when the caterpillar thought the world was ending, it turned into a butterfly*. Finally, a loud bump sounded in the fireplace. It was the invitation! She had done it!

Emme's parents were so proud of her that they decided to have a Surprise Dinner. They all sat at the table with empty plates and cups, and everyone closed their eyes and imagined what they would like to eat. You could be lucky or unlucky – that was the Surprise. Poor Jess ended up with Brussel sprouts with jam, but Holly shared her peanut butter carrots with her.

Emme watched the stars from her bunk bed that night and felt very proud of herself.

CHAPTER SIX

Today was the big day! Emme woke up early, as if it was her birthday. To pass the time, she made her family a nice breakfast: pancakes with honey and freshly squeezed fairberry juice.

When the rest of the Dixons finally woke up, they all sat down and ate together. Her mum took off her pager so it wouldn't buzz during family time, even though she was about to start a new mission in work.

After breakfast, Emme went upstairs to put on her graduation outfit – a unicorn top and a sparkly pink skirt. It was a warm morning, so she put on sandals and tied her hair up in a high ponytail with a silk ribbon. She felt very wise and grown-up! She'd dreamt of today since she was a baby fairy learning how to fly with her mum.

As it was a very special day, her parents had booked a Butterfly Taxi as a surprise to bring them all to the graduation. Butterflies made great taxis, because they were the most trusted creatures in the fairy world. It was a real treat for the three sisters, as they'd never been on one before.

They flew out of the treehouse to see a beautiful peacock butterfly resting on a branch. She had red wings with six blue spots, and big green eyes that sparkled when she smiled. All the family jumped on. There were tiny seats and seatbelts, so everyone was strapped in nice and tight.

The butterfly glided carefully and gracefully up out of the treehouse and down through Tree Road. As everyone was admiring the view and looking at some tiny birds singing, Holly spotted Ollie and Hugo Barns sunbathing on the grass, just like Harry had told her. Time to put her plan into action. She leaned over the side and dropped a full water bomb on their heads!

They got a terrible fright and jumped up screaming. Ollie started looking around, thinking that a big bird had pooped on his head!

'Yeesssssss!' Holly whispered to herself. 'Bullseye!'

A few minutes later, their Butterfly Taxi gently swooped down and landed outside the school on the soft grass. 'Thank you so much,' they all said, undoing their seatbelts.

There was a big sign that said Graduation
Party, and they walked up the path together.
As they got closer to the building, they began
to hear music, and they followed it down the
corridor and into the hall.

The whole room was decorated like a sky.
The walls were baby blue, and in each corner,
speakers shaped like fluffy clouds were playing
fairy music. Pink umbrellas dangled upside

down from the ceiling, with rainwater pouring

down into puddles. In the centre of the room

was a massive rainbow-coloured slide with lots

of twists and loops.

Mr Gloop, the wizard chef, had done such a

brilliant job that Holly felt bad about calling him

Mr Poop behind his back. The tables were covered

with platters overflowing with fruit like papaya and pink pineapples. In a massive bowl, there was fizzy silver popcorn and sticky buns. The blue toffee apples shone like jewels and the sandwiches were shaped like pots of gold. The purple blueberry ice lollies were in shamrock shapes.

Mr Dixon was in his element! He looked around the room, trying to guess all the ingredients. He even wrote down a few ideas for the *Fairy Good Bake Off*.

As they stood at the entrance, taking it all in, Emme noticed Ms Ava talking to a man in the corner and laughing. She was wearing a shimmering gold dress and her hair was in a long braid with all the colours of the rainbow.

The man with her was wearing a suit. He was very handsome, with brown eyes and long hair in a ponytail, and one of his ears was pierced. There was something very mysterious about him!

Ms Ava saw Emme waving, so she smiled and walked towards them. 'Hello, Emme and everyone,' said Ms Ava to the family. 'You're all so welcome to the graduation. Go and have a wander, get some food and have some fun. I'll be giving out the medals at the presentation later on.' The medals had been designed by a five-hundred-year-old gnome called Ivor Badbreth, and the Dixons admired them as they lay on a table in the centre of the room.

As Ms Ava was talking to the sisters' parents about the traffic congestion on Tree Road, Emme looked to the side, and the mysterious man was no longer there. It was as though he had disappeared into thin air! Maybe she was just going a bit loolah, Emme thought to herself. After all, she had been so excited that she hadn't slept very well. She must be tired.

The girls left their mum and dad to chat with the other parents and headed over towards the slide. Lots of their class were there, all dressed up in beautiful dresses, cool tops that shimmered like rain, and striped leggings. The camels had shown up in matching red dresses and the trolls looked clean, wearing dark suits and shades. The polar bears must have just come from the park because they were in T-shirts and shorts. They looked a bit out of place!

Everyone played on the slide, jumped in the rain puddles, ate the delicious food, drank the fairberry juice and danced around the room, flossing and doing the Secret Fairy Dance. Emme squealed with excitement when The Twisters' new song 'Rainy-Face' came on.

Finally, they heard Ms Ava announce that it was time for everyone to take their seats, as the presentation was about to start. Emme felt a bit giddy, but she waited patiently as Ms Ava gave a speech about how proud she was of the class and how much she had enjoyed teaching them all. She said that she felt a bit sad to see them leave for big school, but that she knew that they were ready for the next stage in their lives.

Then she started calling out people's names.
Emme waited. It felt like there was popcorn
popping in her tummy. Her mum held one of
her hands and Holly held the other. Jess had
hidden some buns in her pocket and was making
a terrible mess at the back of the room!

'**EMME DIXON**!' said Ms Ava.

It was time! Her parents jumped up to clap and give her a big hug. Then, much to her amusement, and her parents' shock, Holly started letting off loud party poppers from her pocket. Emme couldn't help but laugh. Her sister meant well!

Up she walked to the top of the room and onto the stage. 'Well done, Emme,' said Ms Ava, smiling. She leant down and whispered to her. 'You are a very special fairy, and I know that you will do some incredible things with your gifts.' She winked at Emme as if she was planning something.

Emme was grinning from ear to ear as she walked back to take her seat with her gold medal firmly in her hand. She was going to sleep with

it under her pillow tonight, in case Jess tried to 'borrow' it!

The Dixon family said their goodbyes and headed back home on their Butterfly Taxi. Everyone was tired but happy, except Jess, who felt a bit sick from scoffing all the buns. She decided that it would be rude to get sick on the beautiful butterfly and ruin Emme's day! She let out a quiet **burp** as they flew up the trunk of the tree and back to their treehouse.

'What's next then, Emme?' asked Mr Dixon, putting his arm around her.

'I'm not really sure yet,' said Emme, crossing her small fingers behind her back. She knew exactly what her next assignment would be … and she was sure it would be exciting!